"My Sex Is Ice Cream"
The Marilyn Monroe Poems

"My Sex Is Ice Cream"
The Marilyn Monroe Poems

Including

In Her Own Writ

A selection of original poetry
by Marilyn Monroe

Nellie McClung

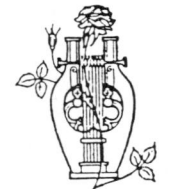

Ekstasis Editions

Canadian Cataloguing in Publication Data

McClung, Nellie
    My sex is ice cream: the Marilyn Monroe poems

    Poems.
    ISBN 0-921215-95-9

    1. Monroe, Marilyn, 1926-1962– Poetry. .I. Title.
    PS8575.C64M9   1996   C811'.54   C96-910123-6
    PR9199.3.M2935M9   1996

Copyright © 1996 Nellie McClung
Cover Design: Richard Olafson

Acknowledgements
The poems by Marilyn Monroe are transcribed by the late Normon Rosten, and used by permission. He passed away last year, 1995. The author would like to thank him and his daughter Patricia Rosten for their assistance. The quote after the preface is from *Marilyn: An Untold Story* by Norman Rosten (New American Library, New York, 1973). The cover photograph is by Lawrence Schiller, taken on the set of *Something's Got To Give.*

Published in 1996 by
Ekstasis Editions Canada Ltd.
Box 8474, Main Postal Outlet
Victoria, B.C. V8W 3S1

Ekstasis Editions
Box 571
Banff, Alberta T0L 0C0

My Sex Is Ice Cream: The Marilyn Monroe Poems has been published with the assistance of a grant from the Cultural Services Branch of British Columbia.

Printed in Canada by Hignell Printing, Winnipeg, Manitoba

for her two

best friends

who loved her,

*Carl Sandburg
& Norman Rosten,
the Brooklyn
poet laureate*

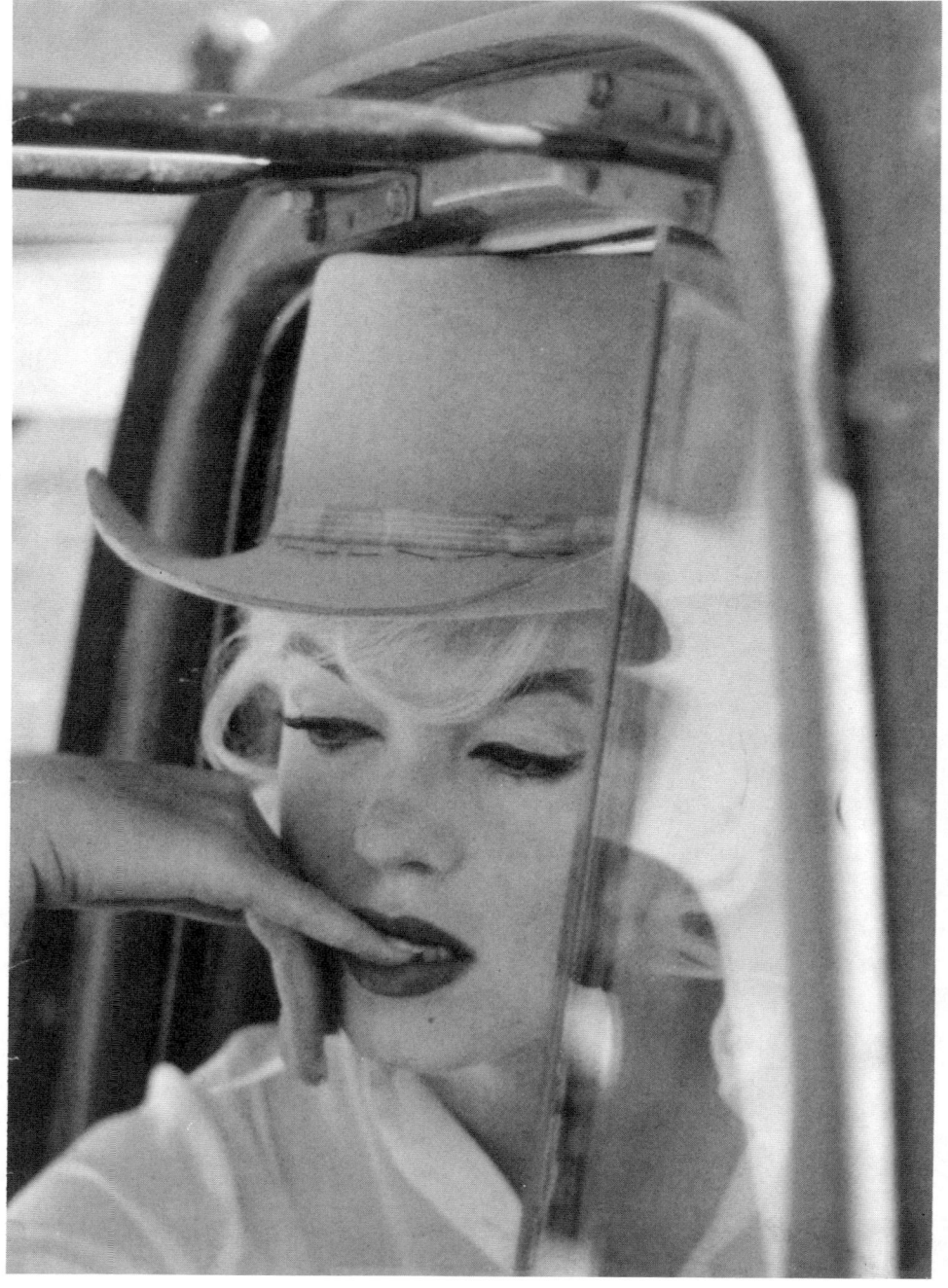

Preface

I first thought about Norma Jean when my aunt Irene said to me one day when I was 23 I reminded her of Marilyn Monroe. At that time I was quite pretty... You can tell from Marilyn's photographs she grew more beautiful as she grew older. Like most other women, my looks faded. She was 3 years older than me, born in 1926.

I began to see all her movies. Who can forget her in *Bus Stop*, *Some Like It Hot*, *The Prince and the Showgirl* and *The Misfits*. The next thing I heard about her was when she was in Banff filming *River of No Return* (which she called "a cowboy film"). She made headlines when she was turned away from the Banff Springs Hotel for going to dinner in slacks. Yeah, Marilyn!

We have a number of things in common. Like her, I feel nearer to animals than humans, I have a genius for picking wrong men, childless too, went through my party girl years, can't cook, flirted with suicide and was hospitalized. I'm a Celtic dreamer too, dreaming of Olwyn, the Irish dream. Some days I feel I can tackle the world: other days I feel as fragile as Norma Jean. Unlike her there is no mystery of illegitimacy. I had a strong family background and a very happy childhood. Like her I have a driving ambition to be a writer.

Marilyn wrote talented poetry which her friend Carl Sandburg said was quite good. You can follow the development of her talent until she wrote the final haunting poem "Don't cry little doll, don't cry. I think I want to die" A friend told me they once saw a self-portrait she had done that was quite beautiful.

Norman Rosten, the Brooklyn poet laureate, was her friend and saw her through Arthur Miller and other lovers. She was a joy to be in the same world with, bringing beauty, humour and grace to everything she touched. One cannot imagine doing the poems of Jackie Kennedy, Sophia Loren, or Elizabeth Taylor. There was not that sheer beauty of Soul, and rare innocence. Goodnight, Pretty Woman. "*Buenos noches Linda Muher.*"

Nellie McClung, *Casa Contenta, Vancouver, 1996*

> *She would often hand me a scrap of paper with something written on it and ask, "Do you think this is poetry? Keep it and let me know." Or she'd send a scribbled sheet in the mail asking for criticism. I would always encourage her. The poems were, in the best sense, those of an amateur; that is, they pretended to be nothing more than an outburst of feeling, with little or no knowledge of craft. But the poet within her—and one existed—found a form for her purpose.*
>
> *As is often the case with poetry, it is a kind of therapy, and what came of these imperfect scribblings must have surprised her. There are echoes of struggle, search, and torment, with origins we can only guess at.*

Norman Rosten, *Marilyn: An Untold Story*
   (New American Library, New York, 1973)

"My Sex Is Ice Cream"

"She was a girl who knew how to be gay, even when she was feeling sad, and lonely, and that's important you know..."
Marilyn to an interviewer about acting Sadie Thompson

"My men expect so much of me because of the sex-symbol image," she once said. "They expect bells to ring, but I can't live up to it."

My Song

my sex is ice cream
come to me
there's a tender dream
to share
I'm every man's love affair
with America
sweet angel of sex
sugar of sex
generous
adventuresome
forgiving
humorous
compliant
& tender
I ask no price
I'm waiting between the sheets
a rare sexy morning
take me
I'm easy
I'm happy
child-goddess nymphet
child of the universe
my skin glowing
my undergarment
I'm an angel of sex, you bet
& as the poet says
when you drink a beer to me
(even yet)
let a smile come to your lips.

(after Norman Mailer)

Born To Hollywood
June 1, 1926

I discovered myself

year of Valentino's death
sound was coming in
"Jazz Singer" running on
                        Broadway

Al Jolson
Clara Bow was in "Kid Boots"
Joan Crawford "In Paris"
Greta Garbo & Gloria Swanson

John Barrymore & John Gilbert

I was
named Norma Jean Mortenson
after Norma Talmadge, the
        movie star

Gladys Mortenson, mother
father known (Martin Edward Mortenson?)
& unknown (Stanley Gifford?)

charity ward

I come in all my mother's doubt,
& leave in mystery

G. Stanley Gifford
my mother showed me a picture of him

when I was young

slouch hat
cocked on one side of his head
a little moustache and a smile

he looked kind of like

Clarke Gable, you know, strong and manly
an employee of Consolidated Film Industries

where my mother worked

it seems

I have always been looking for him
25 years later,
I discovered him
a successful dairyman

(Red Rock Dairy)
living in Helmet, California

Put in a call for a visit
but he wouldn't come to the phone

suggested I see his lawyer

when I was born
mothers' co-workers collected $140
for the Los Angeles General Hospital
stud, he never contributed

but I didn't meet him, until
in my early teens

I kept a picture of Gable
on my wall
& lied to my high school friends
that he was my secret father

Grandpa Monroe
he was a descendent

to President Monroe
but all you need know about him
(my mother told me)

is how when she was three

he pulled a pet kitten
out of her arms and threw it

against the wall

enough to drive anyone insane
in later years

Movies

every Saturday at the movies
acting Jezebel
playing Marie Antoinette
saying goodbye to her lover
Tyrone Power
(stood on the bed to be him
weeping farewell to the children
climbing in to the tumbrel, the bed)

generally people called
me "The Mouse" I was so quiet
in a room of people

walking around the
movie stars' home
& planning to be a movie star
when I grow up

Destiny

even in the orphanage lot
across the street
sitting at the window
a repeating flash
repeating flash
forked neon lighting:
RKO

Orphanage

the sign read:
LOS ANGELES ORPHAN'S HOME
I was nine
I'm not an orphan
my mother is alive
someone's making a terrible mistake
I refuse to walk in
they drag me in screaming
centre hall
while I screamed
        I'm not an orphan!
children's faces turning
I am embarrassed and fall silent

years later
a starlet
Bob Slatzer, a friend
spends his last $250
buying presents
for the children
& hurrying over to the orphanage
Christmas eve

But I stayed at the door
I didn't want to go in
as though they could capture me again

A Girl Can Get Lonely

"Divine love has always met and will always meet every human need."
Mary Baker Eddy

I never discuss it
                       but since you ask
waif   born out of wedlock
Shunted through homes like a merry-go-round
the orphanage where we worked for 10 cents a week
         drying dishes
                cleaning toilets
                        washing dishes
Grandma Della smothering me
      with a pillow
              my first known memory
(Will I die someday by suffocation?)
        calling our parents "Mother"
when she wasn't
     my real mother
wandering around singing
                     "Jesus Loves Me"
in homes that laughed
                     while they drank
pushing Lester over
          on a tricycle
                 & getting a spanking
catching whooping cough

Tippy going out for a walk at night
             & not coming back

mother
           gone to the hospital
only I wasn't to learn
     why she was there

  the rape by the boarder
      the cry, the pain, the humiliation

       half-truths
I know they say it wasn't all true
   an act of the imagination
     looking for pity

but to me it was true
& that's what's important

people can be so cruel
they say jealous things about me

she's a somnambulist walking around
ten feet under water

a wall of thick cotton

a sloth

you stick a pin in her
& 80 days later she says "ouch"

most people remember
      only the good things

I remember the bad

Dog, Man's Best Friend
(homage to Tippy)

four blocks to kindergarten
Lester & I & Tippy
black & white

always following
waits around the schoolyard
until recess

until he rolled
once too often
on the neighbour's lawn
& the shot rang out

all Tippy wanted to do
was be friendly
& wait for me
at school

Ana Lower

I adored my aunt
she gave me
                SCIENCE AND HEALTH
& we would go
                    on Sundays
Christian Science Church

Love as God and Love in the Universe

church so still
              peace around you
but I felt I wanted
to take off all my clothes
stir up some interest

Love as God and Love in the Universe

Jim Dogherty

he said I couldn't
cook
after I served him
carrots and peas only
for dinner
        I have too many
        fantasies to be a
        housewife, I guess
        I am a fantasy
once I tried to bring
a cow into the living room
well, it was standing
outside in the rain
so scared lonely
forlorn like me
        just sixteen
        I remember
        putting love notes in his
        lunch pail
he was a kind man, a brother

    said 'you'll absolutely
    have to learn to cook, Norma Jean'

"IT"

1. the first I knew
   I had "it" felt loved
   was at the orphanage
   four or five days later
   rain   rain   rain
   which makes me want to run away
   & find my father
   rain rain go away
   come back some other day
   ran away

   a policeman
   back to the orphanage
   taken to Mrs. Dewdney
   expecting to be beaten
   she took me in her arms
   & told me I was pretty
   powder on my nose & chin
   & the mirror:
   there I was all soft as alabaster
   & pretty as mother had been

   2. At Van Nuys High School
      suddenly 12 or 13 boys
      all milling around
      in our yard
      climbing trees & show off
      even the girls paid attention

3. married to Jim
   on Catalina Island
   out for a walk
   men on their knees
   pretending to call
   to Muggsie
       (I must wear tighter sweaters & shorts
       Perhaps try weight-lifting for my breasts
       Ask Jim to bring the bells home
       Where do you think I'd be if I
       hadn't gotten whistles?)

   when any of the boys
   try to make conversation
   I raise my hand
   with my wedding band
   then smile
   just to show there are no
   hard feelings

4. it's a game/fun/exhilarating
   I never enter a room
   without meeting that
   look from the men
   & when I leave I know which
   ones I could have had

It's one of the pleasures of being a woman

    as Catherine Deneuve
   would say
   winding her arms around
   a bottle of Channel No. 5

Animals Are My Best Friends

I am drawn
              to all living things
I spent
      hundreds of dollars

             to save a storm-damaged tree
& mourned its death
I welcome birds
         providing tree houses
                worrying about them
                       in bad weather
my dog was contemplative
          I did my best to make him play
When he rarely did
         antic pirouettes
I would hug and kiss him
         delirious with joy
Soft creatures,
        they need our love and protection
     Where do birds go at night
I like to talk to
        winos on the street
& when I feed the sparrows
    I feel I identify with them

*my roommate
was Shelley Winters,
we were starlets
but with ambition
serious actresses*

*she was very nice
mothered me*

*trying to cook
later, she will say
I was very sweet*

*two honest women
in glittering
Hollywood*

*I liked her
She was a good sport,
fun even then
talented*

Johnny Hyde

he was the first
to treat me like a lady

taught me
      how to talk
      how to walk
      how to dress

I cried when I had to
tell him I couldn't marry
him

they said his heart
attack was my fault

he knew I was a girl
on the way up

Fortune

they laughed
when I said I wanted
to leave photographs of my body
for posterity
but when you have a beautiful body
what should you do with it
but lend it?

Weekend In Mexico

one weekend Bob Slatzer
set off for Tijuana
we walked Rosarita Beach
swam nude in the surf
& downed margaritas
then we went off
to find a lawyer
dodging tourists & Mexican peddlers
we bought a $100 glass ring
I spoke to the Virgin Mary
Jesus Christ & Joseph
in a cathedral
lighting a candle
& asked for forgiveness
& we were married in the lawyer's office
we danced at the Foreign Club
where Rita Hayworth danced
& lived as man & wife
for two days
but I was
waiting for a
phone call from Joe DiMaggio
but then it was over
& we went back to the lawyer
& burned the paper
I cried most of the way home

Natasha

You can't be married
& be a great actress
was pounded into me
by my drama coach
She would always be
on the set insisting on retakes
until it was perfect
Finally we grew apart
A girl has to move on

Hearsay

after all the ballyhoo
(sex goddess,
another Jean Harlow)
what was I really like
in bed?
the word
      comes from Hollywood
not a fireball
sometimes frigid
pleasant in bed
ceremonious like a geisha

that's the word

& lover

      who had not

           been in love

said
"of course, I cannot say
how she was with other men
a little remote with me,
And very friendly, I liked her"

Beyond the grave
I keep my veiled eyes
on the subject

I've Been On A Calendar But Never On Time

for all the fuss
it was only $50
for my car instalment

Tom Kelley said
I was graceful as
an otter
turning sinuously
on crushed red velvet
naturally at home
clothes removed

Anyway, I wasn't wearing
nothing on. I had
the radio on!

so what's a girl
supposed to do?

Hibernate?

Nobody objects to
Goya's naked Maja

Why should they
object to me posing
in the nude?

David Conover

Hey, shutterbug
you found me
at Radioplane
Corporation

photographed me
in my overalls
in 1945

we took a trip
through the Mojave Desert
Mount Whitney
& Death Valley

we found a little
terrier with a wounded
leg and took it to the vets

You gave me $100 for
a modelling course
Down through the
years you were always
there even though
you lived far away
on an island in
British Columbia

Bob Slatzer

a writer
he was reading
Leaves of Grass
when I met him
a starlet
in the casting office

we went down to the beach
& I took off all my clothes
& sat beside him in the sand
through the years he will be
my closest confidante
he will be writing
a book about me

after my death
when he lets it be known
he is writing the book
his office will be broken into
& he will be threatened

suggesting someone high up
connected with my death
doesn't want the book
to be written

Gossip

they say
when I finally
signed the movie
contract,
I said, under my curls,
Good! Now I'll never
have to do another
blow job!

Defend me

They say that
about every
Hollywood
starlet

Hello Marilyn Monroe

Zanuck
    said
        Norma Jean Dougherty
            was too long for a marquee
Lyons knew a
        Marilyn Miller
            Ziegfield follies star
so we decided on
        Marilyn Monroe

I wish I had held out
        for Jeane Monroe
            it was difficult for me
to get used to a whole different
                name
        I had a hell of a
time learning to spell
        Marilyn

Books & I

> *"She seemed to me a thoughtful
> person, a searching person,
> trying to educate herself."*
> Her friend, Jane Russell

I guess I was better off
when I was just

        a dumb blonde
didn't know anything about Dostoevsky/Sandburg/Joyce

when they thought I was
        putting on airs
running around with
a book under my arm
in the studio cafeteria
I was reading *Dodsworth*   *Look Homeward Angel*
    Ulysses   *Psychopathology of Everyday Life*
I Married Adventure
    Robert Service e.e. cummings Yeats
Swann's Way
Goodnight Sweet Prince   *An Actor Prepares*—Stanislavsky
A
    Trumpet In the Dust
        Tamberlane
            Beau James
Letters To A Young Poet
Shoe The Wild Mare
    As A Man Thinketh
The Postman Always Rings Twice
The Brothers Karamazov

& in the *Bible* my favorite passage was:

> *for what it profit a man
> if he shall gain the whole world
> and lose his soul*

Mr. D —
*(The marriage of Americas' All American Girl
to the All American Guy, Joe DiMaggio)*

it started off well

I asked the

king of baseball
my slugger,
how he got
the blue dot
exactly in the centre
of his tie knot

after a silent dinner

he blushed & shook

his head

but a girl gets tired
of watching TV
there's more to life
that's that

anyway more to my life
I need to be a serious actress
nothing and nobody can stand in my way

He just didn't understand how
important it was to me

but he always wanted to
watch television

we were shooting
The Seven Year Itch
on Lexington Avenue
in New York
& bleachers had been

put across the street
for people to watch

I was walking with
Tom Al down the sidewalk
& neither of us knew
a windmachine had been
placed in a subway grating

the machine blows up my skirt
& I never wear underwear

people cheer

I go into a nearby hotel
& put on some panties

Joe says
"if you go out there again
I'm leaving"

"I'm going"
& we do the scene on
film

that was the end of the
marriage

He was a good guy,
He was my slugger.

Legend

A career is born
               in public
                           talent in
                                         privacy

all they know of me
is I'm always late
(I'm never late,
               I'm just later)
what matters is what you've got
up on the screen
the art
I guess I live
by the mirror
but die by the clock
I once wore a railroad conductor's
watch   but it didn't help
my fights with the studio
at an age of $50,000 a year
I brought in 250 million at the
box office
it's a statistic to show a board
of directors
a return of 500 to 1
later I was getting $100,000 when
Elizabeth Taylor was getting $1 million
for *Cleopatra*

Sleeping in Chanel No. 5
having secrets of makeup
no one has learned
I've had my jaw strengthened
& nose trimmed

14,000 photographs

47 more takes for a single line

they said I would pour for hours

over the photos
I don't want to be the
highest paid movie star
in the world   when I am old
in a rocking chair I may
not have a roof over my head

I want memories
of having been a real actress
I want to be a comedienne
I don't want to make money

I just want to be wonderful

Some Like It Hot

they say
it is my greatest film
Tony Curtis said
it was like kissing Hitler

On a good day I am
two hours late on the set
on a bad day six

46 takes for a oneliner
30 movies all-told
as I get better
the other stars get worse

walking off the stage

to consult with Paula Strasberg

But I am perfectionist   I am the star
Fuck you, Tony!

& on the set
I was reading
Tom Paine's *The Rights of Man*
The communists
They're for the people
aren't they?

Monchan *(sweet little girl in Japanese)*

Valentino's feet
in the forecourt

at Granan's Chinese theatre
were the only footprints
that fit my feet when I was ten

In Korea I hung out of a plane
holding my feet
waving & blowing kisses
to the soldiers below

the breeze & soldiers waving

was something I'll never forget

It was the highlight of my life

I was considered

as a bride for

Prince Rainier

Give me two days alone with him

I said & he'll want to marry me
Mike Todd had me ride on a pink elephant

to Madison Square Garden

Likeness 50 feet tall
front of State Theatre Building
New York

for 7 Year Itch
my white skirt blowing above my legs

meeting Kruschev

& then I sang that song for

President Kennedy

In my red spangled dress
on his birthday
My most cherished
ambition is to do a
movie with Charlie Chaplin

Payne Whitney Clinic

I'm my mother's daughter
grandmother
mothers
uncle
all brought into

insane asylum
ghosts

metal doors

bars on the window
what are you doing to me

what kind of place is this

they are looking at me through the peephole
well, if I am insane

I'll act insane
rip off all my clothes
give them their money worth
somebody get me out of here

Just like the orphanage

like an animal in a zoo
an object of curiosity
for every passing person
who want to look through the glass pane
what I was always afraid of

is happening to me now

Joe!!!!

get me out

Arthur Miller

Time called us
        The Owl & The Pussycat
married to him five years
     let him write

his damn play about me
     exorcising his guilt
like an ant
     under surveillance

               my fall
                        my drugs
               my booze
        my attempts at suicide

my silence is eloquent

The Misfits

Arthur writes scripts
John shoots ducks

first Arthur screwed up the script
now I am screwing up the script
Arthur doesn't know

whether the horse should be up or down
I think we would keep the scene with my nude
breasts in bed
John cuts it out
Clark dies without seeing his son

Monty is buying into the

Del Monte grapefruit business

Film costs $4 million
& Arthur & I are at the
breaking point

the film that would bestow
on my soul, the greatest

American film star, by the greatest
American dramatist
fizzles out in real life

We are the misfits

Dame Edith

Dame Edith Sitwell
when she came to America

the person who she wants to see
was me. ME!

I was wearing a green dress
She said I looked
like a daffodil
they thought we'd never get along
but we took a liking
to each other immediately

at lunch

we discussed Rudolph Steiner
the *Course of My Life*
which I was reading
& then danced around the room
the earth dance for Rudolph

Another person
who took to me
was the Danish-African author
Countess Blixen
(Isak Dineson)

Lee Strasberg

I call Strasberg in London
with Olivier
from the set of *The Prince and the Showgirl*
my voice burns wires

Lee, how do you become sexy?

What do you do to be sexy?

Let's Make Love

Our 3 month fling   Yves Montand
just a school girl crush
as I said to the press
he was going back to Simone, his wife

he bragged to his friends she'll be anywhere
I say on time
She's got so she'll do

whatever I ask her to do

on the set

everyone is amazed at her co-operation

& she's constantly looking to me
for approval

it seems I'm always running into
people's unconsciousness

Television Appearance Before 300 Million Around The World

my command performance
had the dress made
red sequin number
strapless sheath
backless, skin tight
two hours of makeup

backstage at the Madison Square Gardens

green room

meeting the President
(our relationship
not yet uncovered
by the press)

with Isidore Miller
my ex-father-in-law

peeking out here
between the curtains
audience excited
there they calling
Miss Marilyn Monroe
the spotlight

Miss Marilyn Monroe! spotlight
the late Miss Marilyn Monroe!
walking out

clapping   clapping

whistles
catcalls
Marilyn!
Marilyn!
Marilyn!
Marilyn!

clapping died down
look towards Jack
in the dais
spirit of mischief

Happy Birthday to you
Happy Birthday to you

Happy birthday, Mr. President
Happy Birthday to you

hush
clapping   cheers
they love me
they love me
rush of love
& then the President
laughing

gallant
Now I can retire
from politics
I've been sung to
by Miss Monroe

It's a
It's a long way, baby
from the
Los Angeles orphanage

*Jacqueline Kennedy phoned
& told me that if I
married Jack, I'd have to
live in the White House*

*that didn't make me too
happy—*

Notes

I'm the talk
of the shop girls

because I wear nothing
underneath

at night to make up

I sleep in my brassiere

(it keeps my breasts from
sagging)

Pretty as a bird up high
let me be free

or let me be free
let me fly

Frank Sinatra

after our love affair

he gave me a white poodle
the sweetest little thing
I called it "MAF" (short for Mafia)

that dog meant more to me than

any mink or diamond bracelet

of all the men I have known
I'd have to list him
the most fascinating

My Inner Life

a girlfriend will say

I had 12 abortions

Is this true,

or was she fabricating?

Only I know

for sure

Hindsight

just as films are my genius
for my talent
is my genius
for picking the wrong man

I know now

I should have married

Joe (again) or Mailer
they show by their books
their roses

they truly love me

I'd be alive
Still with you
I'd be 66
in 1992
Zounds!

understand my career

understand my sexiness as an art

love me for myself
what I am

they would have seen me through

I never give parties

I don't want my friends

getting together &

talking about me

The telephone is the one
friend I can count on
when I am lonely, upset
or need advice
Besides its easier to talk
than write letters

My telephone bills come
to $11,000 a month

I like to write
poems when
I am depressed &
lonely
I show them to
Carl & Norman,
my scribblings

it's 3:00 a.m.
in Brooklyn
must phone Norman
& tell him about
the birth of
four kittens
at my house in
Beverly Hills

easy birth but
was worried
two orange/two
grey & white

so darling
        so forlorn

I talk for an hour
as Norman nods off
several times

"Are you there?"
they're so cute
as sweet as Maf

he tells me gently
he is bored & has to
get off the phone

*dear Norman
my best friend
has to listen to
a lot from me*

he goes back to bed

I stay up all night,

ecstatic

*I don't want people
to dislike me   That's
something I can't stand
You know that's my weakness
Wanting people to like me
To accept me ....*

The Last Nude Session

On the set of *Something's Got To Give*
the movie
called for
a nude swimming scene

with several photogs

shooting freely
I toss off the skin tight suit

& do a dog paddle across the pool

they call me a nymphet

in excitement

first nude pictures in 14 years
contract drawn up

pictures splashed across the world

chin on foot on pool deck

cameras whirring

making $1,000,000 for the photogs

anyway, Botticelli worked with nudes

mode

they say I am
         narcisstic/
  so be it
but I love to
admire myself
naked in the mirror

(who wouldn't)
I fall in love easily
& fall out hard

I still have
         the same dream
    my recurring dream/

about being nude

I'm standing in the church
listening to a sermon

     & all of a sudden
I stand up

     I'm perfectly nude/

the people all just stare at me/
    & that other dream too/
with me running
around nude
in a grassy cemetery/
          at night/

my drink is Dom Perignon
    (champagne at $27.50 a bottle)
a drink with a pal
bathing in Chanel No. 5
playing my Frank Sinatra records

mostly I like to wear
shirts, slacks, a sweater
         with sandals

(the better to take off)
& run through

the sand and surf
in barefeet
it's important

to be free/ you know?

GOODBYE NORMA JEAN

reinstated on set
of *Something's Got To Give*

last seen
by the neighbours
in the backyard
in the evening
throwing the ball
for
      "Maf"

a visit by RFK & a doctor

who gives me an injection

Mexicali House

I've always lived in
                    apartments
so this is my first real home
a mission style house
white stucco walls
casement windows

Spanish style
all Mexican furniture
bought on trips to Mexico
white inside walls
white rug from India

Mexican glass chandelier
mission style chests & carvings
Chinese carvings

my greatest pride
            is the kitchen

robins' egg blue refrigerator
all tiles flown in from Mexico

oval swimming pool
maybe I'll learn to swim yet
although I was never in it

secluded garden of bamboo
        & Mexican pots

I cried when I signed the
contract/ I never thought I
would buy a house alone/

my friends will say I
        had so much to live for
was excited about my house

that it must have been
accidental suicide or murder

it couldn't have been suicide
I would have left Joe a note

they will find barbituates
in my stomach
my hand on the telephone

RFK

he said I could never remember
the things he told me
so I started to write down
what he said in a little red diary

& reviewing the notes before
I saw him each time

$209 on long distance calls
to the Justice Department

my call tolls erased by someone with power
after my death
                (the witches wheel of
Chappaquadick)

it was not his finest hour

Motif?

RFK also told me

he "could have people done away with"

I put this in my diary

& told Bob Slatzer

he had promised to get a divorce

from his wife & marry me

when this didn't happen
I threatened to call a press conference

& denounce him

& went around telling everybody

Bob said it wasn't very smart of me

Years later, someone
will try & sell
my little red diary

Traveller, Farewell

August 5, 1962
Fifth Helena Drive
Brentwood, California

What am I afraid of?
Why am I so afraid?
I am afraid & I must not be

the clicks on the telephone

my ending as ambiguous as my life
I want to sleep for a long, long time
Mustn't go to sleep now   Try to stay awake

say goodbye to the President for me
say goodbye to the President

the cold, the cold

I'll phone RFK again
phoning me to do a party
                with some hookers
what does he think I am?
I'm tired of this whole thing
                of being a plaything

The pillow, the pillow
Take the pillow away Della

drifting   drifting   drifting

Tippy, my unknown father, Della & Gladys
in the insane asylums

ghosts from my past

I feel terrible & I am about to jump out
             of my skin

they used to say when you grew up
you wouldn't feel things (But it isn't
so) It's worse

they will say I was found nude
with a lover (no brassiere on
like when I am alone)

drifting   *drifting*   *drifting*

I must talk to the President
I'll phone again now
....click....click....click....click
the housekeeper will find me with
my hand on the telephone
I am smothered
Truth will have it's day in my death & life

drifting   *drifting*   *drifting*

cold   *cold*   *cold*

drifting   *drifting*   *drifting*

dark   *dark*   *dark*

I lean on God today

Postscript

even in death
they will be taking
bites out of me

a shrewd young woman
in Hollywood will hold
out for $25,000

for the plot next to mine
in Memorial Park

Joe will want
to be buried there
next to me but
can't raise the money

I'll tell you
what to do   it's simple

C'mon Joe
just move my
remains
from the crypt   Be smart
then we
can be side
by side, dear

you were the husband
that always loved me
in Life, in Death

sending a dozen red

roses every day
a broken heart

my slugger

Madonna

what is it with
this crazy kid
Madonna?

running around
telling everyone
she's me reincarnated
(not too likely)

& buying the crypt
next to me in the
mausoleum (better
it were Joe!)

I was always a lady
about sex, treated it
with humour, I never
made blue movies,

never expostulated the Cross,
calling it "sexy"
never masturbated on
stage, never vulgarized
myself

Get lost, Madonna!
I don't want
to go into Eternity
with you by
my side—

Young David

RFK will tell
his son, David

stories about me
& young David

will identify with
me & come often

to visit my grave
ending his own life

                      with
an overdose

his life entwined
ironically with

mine

Occult

a starlet
when Criswell
predicted
I would be
the most famous
blonde in the world

years later he said
he knew my determination
to be an actress

I'm a Gemini
Geminis have two
continuously changing
sides
one day I'm happy
the next day
sad, quiet, cold, unfriendly

Geminis make few friends
quickly but drop them
just as easily
searching for someone
or something new
a hunger for knowledge
use charm instead of
discussion

Geminis lack concentration
are highly sensitive
highstrung
frequently fall in love
sometimes too easily
marry husbands
who are constant

In Hollywood
they will hold a seance
for me
& ask for a sign
the fountain will
suddenly bubble over
& they will know
I am around

*someday a Japanese
astronomer will
discover a new shining
star twinkling in the
galaxy & people
will name it after me*

*then I will always
be near you the better
to look after you
twinkling with
joy*

who was I calling?
it doesn't matter

sometimes I think
it would be easier

not to reach old age

to die young

but then you'd never
be complete
would you?

you'd never really know
                            yourself

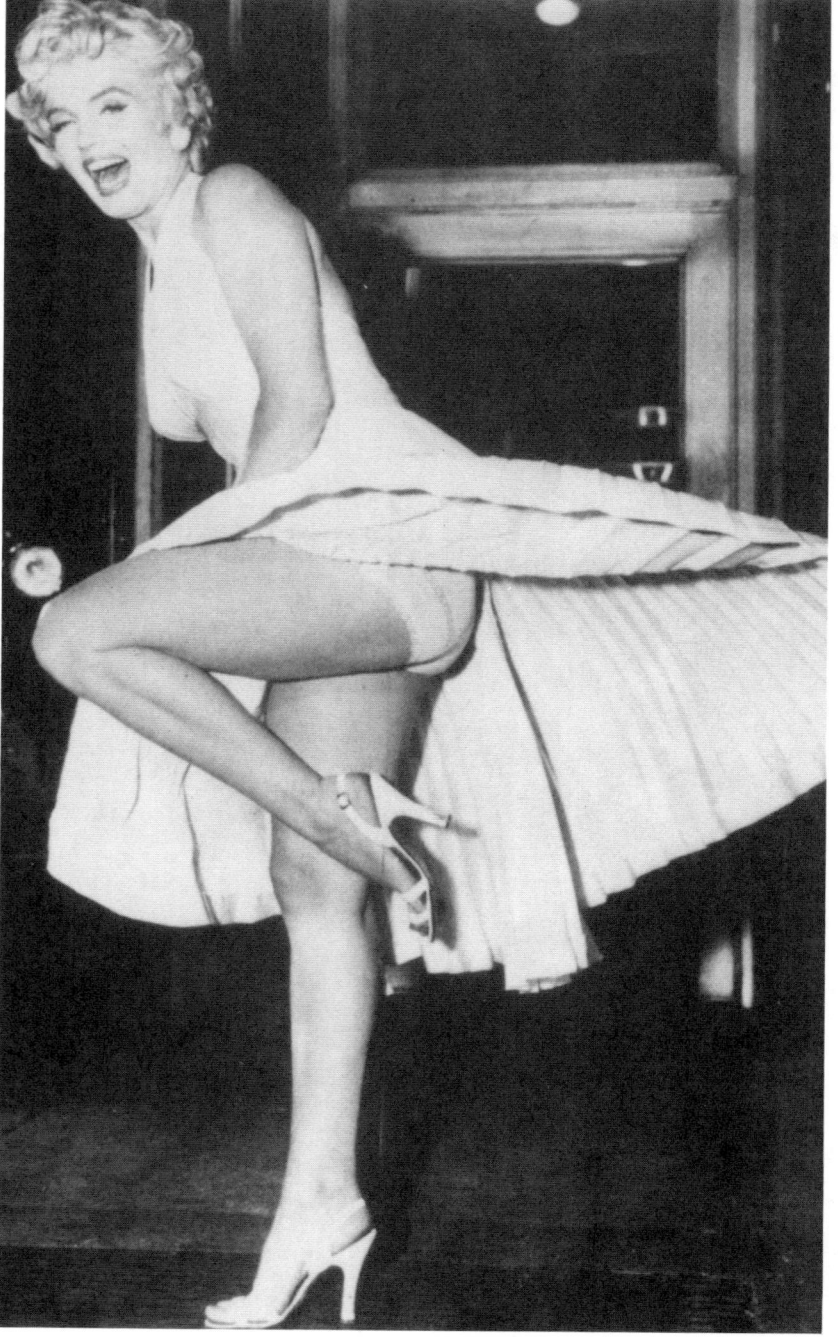

Appendix:

In Her Own Writ:
The Selected Poems of Marilyn Monroe

Transcribed from her Notebooks
by Norman Rosten

(with additional commentary)

From time to time
I make it rhyme
but don't hold that kind
of thing
against
me —
Oh well what the hell
so it won't sell
what I want to tell —

is what's on my mind
taint Dishes
taint Wishes
its thoughts
flinging by
before I die
and to think
in ink

Night of the Nile — soothing —
darkness — refreshes — Air
Seems different — Night has
No eyes nor no one — silence —
except to the Night itself

thinner than a cobweb's thread
sheerer than any —

but it did attach itself
and held fast in strong winds
and sin[d]ged by (?) leaping hot fires
life — of which at singular times
I am both of your directions —
somehow I remain hanging downward the most
as both of your directions pull me

Life —
I am of both your directions
Existing more with the cold frost
Strong as a cobweb in the wind
Hanging downward the most
Somehow remaining
those beaded rays have the colors
I've seen in paintings — ah life
they have cheated you

I.

I left my home of green rough wood,
a blue velvet couch.
I dream till now
A shiny dark bush
Just left of the door.

Down the walk
Clickity clack
As my doll in her carriage
Went over the cracks —
"We'll go far away."

II.

Don't cry my doll
Don't cry
I hold you and rock you to sleep
Hush hush I'm pretending now
I'm not your mother who died.

III.

Help Help
Help I feel life coming closer
When all I want is to die.

I stood beneath your limbs
and you flowered and finally clung to me
and when the wind struck with ... the earth
and sand— you clung to me

"I used to write poetry sometimes but usually I was depressed those times. The few I showed it to (in fact two people) said that it depressed them. One of them cried but it was an old friend I'd known for a long time."
Marilyn to Norman Rosten

"Marilyn referred to poetry quite often. Her friends thought she was joking when she admitted to writing some of it herself. Actually she did try her hand at verses. Poetry is often a kind of therapy and what came out of these imperfect scribblings must have surprised her."
Norman Rosten

Dear Marilyn:
Regrets and sorrow here among us good friends over the latest report of very hard luck incident (possibly a brief hospitalization). When convenient don't fail to send me those poems of which no one else has a copy except our friend Norman Rosten. All who met you here send love,

Ever yours,
Carl. (Sandburg)

"Marilyn was an incredible person...the most marvellous I have ever worked with and I have been working for 29 years. But she went over the fringe. Playing a scene with her, it was like an escalator. You'd do something and she'd catch it, and it would go like that, just right."
Montgomery Cliff

"Don't mention that woman to me!"
—Marilyn's mother in Florida after her release from 40 years in a state asylum.

"She was always playing as close to the edge as she could with suicide but I don't think she went over voluntarily."
Arthur Miller

"Marilyn will live forever to be seen by future generations who will probably appreciate her a little more."
John Huston

"I once heard of a man who had told a head-hunter in Africa that he had come from America, and the savage broke into a smile, clapped his hands and said: "America—Marilyn Monroe."
Wildred Hyde-White, British actor

"She was beautiful, and her loveliness was not entirely human. She seemed lit from within, like the holy figures in certain Renaissance paintings."
Francine Prose

"To me she was a little girl lost."
Patte B. Batham

"Marilyn was the Venus of the 20th century culture. She & her fame will not be forgotten any more than Botticelli's Venus."
Donald Spotow

Afterword: My Friend Norman

When I was working as a poetry reader in Vancouver at Intermedia Press about twenty years ago—"the fastest reader in the west" they called me—around the office, I got the bright idea of publishing Marilyn Monroe's poems. Henry Rappaport, my publisher who on days when he was waiting to meet his banker would be sitting at his desk with his black Mickey Mouse ears on, to my delight, came out and said "if you can't get them why don't you write them." That's where the germ began. I started to read everything on Marilyn Monroe and found that the poems came easily—this was twenty years ago. I worked so hard on them and then I knew I had to get in touch with Norman Rosten in New York for permisssion to use her real poems at the back of a book. I knew all about New York writers. They wouldn't give me the time of day. So I hesitated to write him. Tennessee Williams had come to Vancouver and I got the bright idea of going down and speaking to him. Maybe he would help me with Norman Rosten. Tennessee staged the *Red Rooster* in Vancouver and the only reason he came to Vancouver was no one else would put on the dismal play. I went down to the Playhouse on my mission and tried to meet him; they practically threw me out after I explained my purpose and they said "just go ahead and write Norman Rosten." Tennessee has a very funny poem about new lovers going to a hotel, having sex in bed, waking up having a cigarette, exchanging stories about past lovers; then one, then the other falls asleep, the cigarette lights up the mattress and the ensuing flames burn down the hotel. So, says Tennessee, new lovers shouldn't go to old hotels. So I took the bull by the horns and phoned New York. When I said I was a writer in Canada, who had written some poems about Marilyn, Norman's clipped accent said "My poems are better." I nodded and hung up.

    Then I sent in my books *Tea With the Queen*, *Baraka*, *Duenda*, and *Pomegranate*. Back came the letter: "I will put up the plaque for you." He is the only person who has ever understood my books.

    My grandmother, Nellie L. McClung, suffragette, has a plaque in the Senate in Ottawa for the Famous Five, women who won the vote. I wanted some plaques too since I do everything she did. Only mine are different. A sign of the times. Mine are going to be at the CPR station in Banff where I would take my sleeping bag and go down and sleep behind the bench in the woman's wash-room while learning to be an artist at the Banff School of Fine Arts in 1963. "My suicide" was very imaginative when I swam from Ottawa to Hull in an attempt to become a Mystic, nearly drowning at the Eddy Match factory in the same year. And finally at the United Nations in New York where I went in 1971 to stop the Vietnam War.

My father never read my grandmother's books; my husband has never read mine. I would write Norman long letters. He was too wise to commit himself on paper. He would just write back cryptic funny replies. "What's this?" he said. And in my books *Tea with the Queen* I have written "and in the dark basement, when you had to go down to the apple box for a Kiwanis in the corner by the furnace there was a special procedure. Mother sitting in the livingroom, taking her role seriously, never laughing at you. The first step calling out 'hello' she answering 'hello.' You on the second step 'hello', the third step 'hello', and so on until you could run and grab an apple free of the Dark Bogeyman, up the stairs again. And then run with the wind again for the rest of the afternoon." And once many years later I came across a line in a poem:

and after you had gone down the longest stair.
And then I knew others had played The Game.

For everyone goes through the same experiences and if there is an undercurrent, a common denominator, then that is it.

And that is what these chapters are all about.

Then Norman sent me his beautiful poem about going down the longest stair. Then he wrote and asked me if I could get him a drug in Canada to send him (illegal in the US) for his wife Hedda's asthma. I went to the doctor and kept sending him the drug tablets. He really liked me because it helped at the last. Then she died, a beautiful Danish woman I would like to have met. We kept writing and I planned to visit him for a few days: "don't bring your ten friends when you come" was his remark.

When the market crashed in 1987, not having any money to lose, I took a special delight in going around asking everyone how much they lost. My brother a judge in Edmonton, six years my junior, told me was "decimated." I think he lost a cool million. I asked Norman: "I don't know," he said wittily on the telephone. "I think I left it in an old shoe-box somewhere."